Bear's Picture

WRITTEN BY

Daniel Pinkwater

ILLUSTRATED BY

D. B. Johnson

HOUGHTON MIFFLIN COMPANY

BOSTON 2008

For David Nyvall
— D. P.

For Ann and George
— D. B. J.

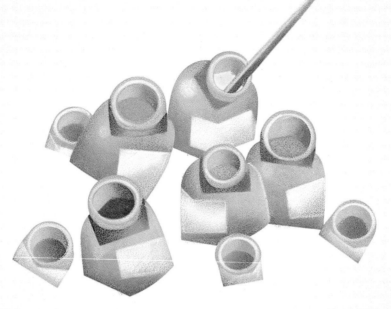

First Houghton Mifflin edition 2008.
Text copyright © 1972 and © renewed 2000 by Daniel Pinkwater
Illustrations copyright © 2008 by D. B. Johnson

www.houghtonmifflinbooks.com

The text of this book is set in Bodoni.
The illustrations are mixed media.

Library of Congress Cataloging-in-Publication Data

Pinkwater, Daniel Manus, 1941–
Bear's picture / written by Daniel Pinkwater ; illustrated by D. B. Johnson. — 1st Houghton Mifflin ed.
p. cm.
Summary: A bear continues to paint what he likes despite criticism from two passing gentlemen.
ISBN-13: 978-0-618-75923-1 (hardcover)
ISBN-10: 0-618-75923-9 (hardcover)
[1. Bears—Fiction. 2. Painting—Fiction.] I. Johnson, D. B. (Donald B.), 1944- ill. II. Title.
PZ7.P6335Be 2008
[E]—dc22

2007015149

Printed in China
WKT 10 9 8 7 6 5 4 3 2

A bear wanted to paint a picture.

First he made an orange squiggle.
Then he had a look at it.
"I believe it wants some blue," said the bear.
And he painted some blue.

Then the bear saw a rainbow and put that in too.

Two fine, proper gentlemen, out for a walk,
came upon the bear.
"Look here," said the first fine, proper gentleman,
"a bear painting a picture."

"Bears can't paint pictures," said the second fine,
proper gentleman.

"Why not? Why can't a bear do anything he likes?" asked the bear.

"Because . . ." said the first fine, proper gentleman.
"Because . . ." said the second fine, proper gentleman.
"Bears aren't the sort of fellows who can do whatever
they like," they both said.

"Besides," said the first fine, proper gentleman,
"that is a silly picture."
"Nobody can tell what it is supposed to be," said
the second fine, proper gentleman.

"I can tell," said the bear,
adding some green splotches.

"Ah," said the first fine, proper gentleman.
"Ah," said the second fine, proper gentleman. "Is it
a butterfly? It looks a little like a butterfly."

"No," said the bear, mixing just the right kind of yellow.
"It is not a butterfly."

"Ah," said the first fine, proper gentleman.

"Ah," said the second fine, proper gentleman.

"Is it a clown? It looks a little like a clown."

"No," said the bear, putting in some purple parts.
"It is not a clown."

"Then what is it a picture of?" shouted the
first and second fine, proper gentlemen.

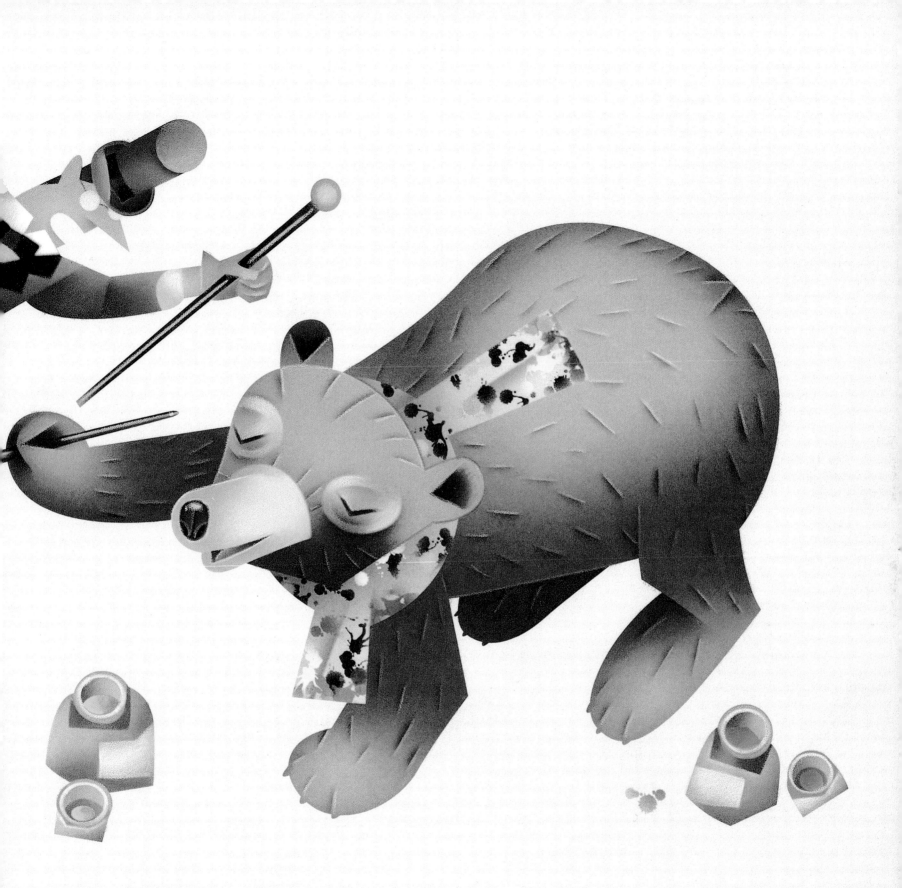

"It is a honey tree," said the bear.
"It is a cold stream in the forest."

"It is a hollow log filled with soft leaves
for a bear to keep warm in all winter long.
It is a field of flowers."

"It doesn't look like any of those things to us,"
said the two fine, proper gentlemen.

"It doesn't have to," said the bear.
"It is MY picture."

The two fine, proper gentlemen went away saying,
"Bears are not the sort of fellows to paint pictures."

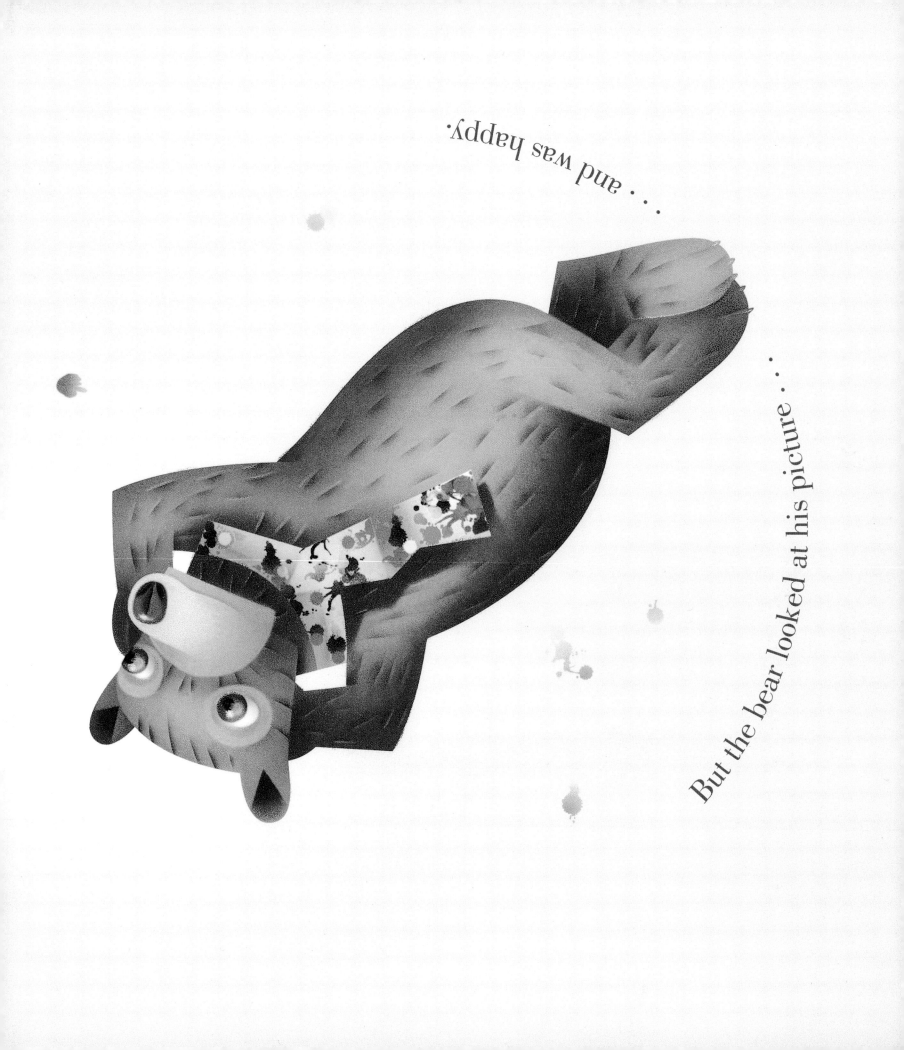

But the bear looked at his picture . . .

. . . and was happy.